To my dear friend Hector

Ed Vieira

Ali and the Tree

Written by Edward T. Vieira, Jr.

Illustrated by Lisa Delaney

Ali and the Tree

ISBN-13: 9798424638732

First Valerius Publishing Edition 2022

For permission requests, email:

edward.t.vieira@gmail.com

Ed dedicates this book to his childhood friend, Steve.

Lisa dedicates this book to her newest grandson, Elias.

"My mom's going to paint my bedroom. I wonder if she'll let me pick the colors," said Teal to Ali.

"So, she's going to actually paint your room, Teal?" asked Ali.

"Very funny. A painter will do it," said Teal.

"Uh-huh," mumbled Ali, wishing Teal would take better care setting the table for tea and cookies.

4

Although it was hot outside, it was cool inside the playhouse. Shade from a nearby apple tree kept things comfortable. Suddenly, they saw Ali's neighbor, Mr. Bacon, drive into his driveway.

After noticing apples on the ground, Mr. Bacon walked toward the apple tree near the playhouse and thinking out loud said, "This tree's a pain in my neck. I'm always rakin' apples. Enough's enough."

He then spotted Ali and Teal through one of the playhouse windows and said, "Don't you kids eat any of these ground apples. They're rotten and will make you sick."

Mr. Bacon went inside his barn. Ali, with Teal closely behind, slowly walked out of the playhouse eyeing the barn.

After a few moments, he returned and loudly said to his wife, who was in the window, "I'm going to get rid of that apple tree tomorrow morning. I'm going right in the barn, get my axe, and chop it down. Come winter, we'll be glad for the firewood."

11

Ali could not move. A tear immediately slipped down her cheek. *No more tree*, thought Ali. Teal went home.

That evening at the dinner table, Ali told her family what Mr. Bacon said. Everyone at the table thought that the tree would be gone soon--- everyone except Ali.

After dinner, Ali went out to play. Ali knew that, every Friday evening, Mr. and Mrs. Bacon went out for supper. They would not be gone for very long.

Once outside, Ali paused for several moments and then ran over to the Bacons' barn, which was never locked. She struggled to pull the heavy squeaky door open just far enough so that she could squeeze through the opening. She found the axe against the back wall. Touching it made Ali nervous. It was very heavy and nearly as tall as her. She gripped the axe so tightly with both hands that her knuckles turned white. She could feel her heart beating. As she dragged it clearly across the yard to her garage, she had to stop twice to catch her breath. She finally got it into the garage and hid it behind a bench.

That morning, Ali felt tired and badly because of what she did. She thought about running away, but decided it wasn't a good idea. She went out into the playhouse and noticed that the barn door was wide open. She could hear noise. Mr. Bacon was searching for something and she knew what it was. He left the barn and stormed into the house.

Ali, who was afraid and about to cry, felt as if she were going to explode. She ran into her garage and dragged the axe under the apple tree where she rested it against the tree. She then ran into the playhouse and took a deep breath.

Mr. Bacon returned and noticed the axe under the tree. He scratched his head as he stared at it. He grabbed it looking up at the tree.

23

Ali had to tell him what she did. There was a long silence before she walked over to him. "Mr. Bacon, I took your axe and hid it. I didn't want you to chop down the tree. I know that it's your tree, and you can do what you want with it. I'm sorry," she said looking down and in a sad voice.

Mr. Bacon looked at her and said nothing. After what seemed like a long time, he said, "I accept your apology."

Ali nodded.

"And you learned something here. Right?" he asked.

Ali nodded again, "Yes sir."

Mr. Bacon looked at the tree swaying in the breeze and then at Ali. "This old tree means that much to you?" he asked.

The answer was in her eyes.

"I suppose the tree isn't all that bad. I don't care for apples myself. But, they don't bother me until they mess up my yard." Mr. Bacon gave a half smile.

Ali looked at the ground under the tree. The apples that were scattered across the grass weren't as pretty as the ones still hanging. An idea crossed her mind. "I could pick them up for you," she said with enthusiasm.

Mr. Bacon stared at her and said, "I suppose if I didn't have to look at the apples on the ground for too long, the ones in the tree could stay. Maybe if you and I work together, it won't be such a big job every now and again. Well? Is it a deal?" He stretched out his hand.

Ali shook his hand eagerly, "It's a deal."

28

Ali knew that if the tree could talk, she would tell all of
the birds that perched on her branches about her good
friend Ali, and how she saved her from Mr. Bacon's axe.

The End.

Made in the USA
Middletown, DE
23 June 2022